W9-BJJ-681

爆

BAKUGAN
BATTLE BRAWLERS
NEW VESTROIA

NEW VESTROIA HANDBOOK

By Tracey West

SCHOLASTIC INC.
NEW YORK   TORONTO   LONDON   AUCKLAND
SYDNEY   MEXICO CITY   NEW DELHI   HONG KONG

ISBN 978-0-545-13122-3

12 11 10 9 8 7 6 5 4 3 2   10 11 12 13 14 15/0

Printed in the U.S.A.
First printing, January 2010

MASTER THE WORLD OF BAKUGAN™

Every Bakugan brawler knows that training never stops. You've got to keep practicing and learning new things if you want to be the best.

This guidebook is designed to help you be the best brawler you can be. Inside, you'll find info about the New Vestroia™ Bakugan and what they're like on the battlefield. You'll learn how to master the new rules of New Vestroia. You'll also meet some of the best Bakugan brawlers in the universe. Some are good guys, some are bad guys, but they've all got what it takes to be champions.

Make sure you check out the last pages of this guidebook, too. There you can enter data about your own Bakugan team.

Add this guidebook to your arsenal of tools: your gauntlet, your cards, and your Bakugan, of course. Now you've got everything you need to master the world of Bakugan.

LET'S BRAWL!

WELCOME TO NEW VESTROIA

You remember how it all began . . . a portal between Earth and a mysterious universe called Vestroia opened up. Bakugan cards fell through the portal, and Dan and his friends found them and created the Bakugan game.

But Dan and the other Battle Brawlers soon learned that Bakugan was more than just a game. A Dragonoid Bakugan named Naga wanted all the power in Vestroia for himself—even if it meant wrecking Vestroia and Earth in the process. Dan and his friends battled fiercely against Naga's servants. In the end, Naga was defeated thanks to Dan's Bakugan Drago, who made the ultimate sacrifice to save his world.

Peace finally came to Vestroia, and the six planets combined to form one large, beautiful world. The Bakugan there roamed freely once more, freed from their Bakugan balls. But that peace didn't last long. An alien race called the Vestals landed in Vestroia and enslaved the Bakugan, battling with them for their own amusement.

Not all of the Vestals in New Vestroia are evil. A few formed the Bakugan Brawlers Resistance. These brave brawlers know that Bakugan are intelligent creatures that deserve to live freely. They've been fighting the Vexos brawlers, but so far, they're outnumbered.

Then Dan and some of his friends came to New Vestroia, and the Bakugan Brawlers Resistance got the boost that it needed. Together they're working to stop the Vexos and free the Bakugan. There's a lot at stake — now that the power in Vestroia is out of balance, the Bakugan universe faces destruction once more!

MEET THE BAKUGAN BRAWLERS RESISTANCE™

The Vestals believe that Bakugan are toys to be played with. But when one Vestal named Mira learned that Bakugan were intelligent creatures with thoughts and feelings, she vowed to free all the enslaved Bakugan in New Vestroia. With her friends Ace and Baron, Mira formed the Bakugan Brawlers Resistance. Their forces became stronger when Dan, Marucho, and Shun found their way to New Vestroia from Earth.

In order to succeed, the Resistance has to defeat the Vexos, the six top Vestal Battle Brawlers. But getting back the captured Bakugan isn't as simple as winning a battle. The Vestals play with their own rules: The winning Bakugan's power level has to be 500 points higher than the defeated Bakugan in order for the winner to take the loser's Bakugan. That means the Resistance brawlers have to be more than good — they've got to use skill, strength, and strategy to take down the Vexos in a big way every time.

The Bakugan Brawlers Resistance knows the only way to win in the end is to destroy the dimension controllers in each of the Vestals' major cities. Without these machines, the Vestals won't have any power to capture the Bakugan. Destroying the controllers won't be easy. The Resistance has to stick together, or they'll lose the biggest battle of all!

Where there's a Bakugan battle, you're likely to find Dan Kuso. Dan has been involved with Bakugan since the very beginning, when the cards fell from the sky. He and his friend Shun made up the rules to the Bakugan game on Earth.

When Drago came to Earth, he needed someone to help him save Vestroia, and Dan didn't hesitate. He rallied the Battle Brawlers against Masquerade and the other brawlers under Naga's control. Dan's loyalty to Drago never wavered.

Now Dan is determined to help the Bakugan Brawlers Resistance and save New Vestroia. He's still hot-headed and impulsive sometimes, but he never runs out of energy, and he never gives up. Dan usually has a positive effect on his teammates, psyching them up when they're feeling down.

DAN'S DRAGONOID

In order to save Vestroia the first time, Drago brought the two power cores of the universe together, the Silent Core and the Infinity Core. The two combined to form the Perfect Core, with Drago's energy at its center.

But when the Vestals came to New Vestroia, Drago was released from the Perfect Core to save his universe once more. He had to leave some of his energy behind, which made him weaker than before. But that hasn't stopped Drago from helping Dan beat the Vexos, one by one.

MIRA

Mira is the brave and determined leader of the Bakugan Brawlers Resistance. She developed her skills as a brawler competing against other Vestals. Like the others, she thought battling with Bakugan was just a sport — and then one day her whole world changed.

Mira surprised her father, Professor Clay, at the lab where he experimented with Bakugan to make them stronger and better. She knew a little bit about her father's work, but she was shocked to find Hydranoid in his lab being blasted with electric jolts. Then the tortured Bakugan spoke to her, and Mira realized the true horror of her father's work.

Mira formed the Resistance, standing tough against the powerful Vexos brawlers. Her teammates look up to her as a strong leader, but even they don't know the secret worry that Mira carries in her heart. Her brother, Keith, has gone missing, and Mira is anxious to find him. But when the truth about Keith is revealed, will Mira be able to accept it?

MIRA'S WILDA

Mira's Guardian Bakugan is as tough as she is. Wilda is a massive creature made of metal and iron, and she uses her mighty strength to pound opponents into the ground. Mira turns to Wilda in every battle, but the toughest battle Wilda fought was against Altair, a Bakugan created by Mira's father.

SHUN

MASTER OF: VENTUS BAKUGAN
GUARDIAN BAKUGAN: INGRAM

Dan's friend Shun was practicing his ninja moves in the forest when a dimension portal opened up and sucked him into New Vestroia. When he got there, Shun rescued Ingram from being captured by the Vestals.

A grateful Ingram vowed to battle by Shun's side, and Shun devoted himself to freeing the captured Bakugan from that moment on. There is one Bakugan he wants to free most of all: his former Guardian Bakugan, Skyress.

MASTER OF: DARKUS BAKUGAN

GUARDIAN BAKUGAN: PERCIVAL

Ace was one of the best Vestal brawlers around. But when Prince Hydron held tournaments to determine the best brawlers for each Bakugan attribute, Ace stayed away. He had no desire to join the Vexos. "I battle alone. I always have," Ace reasoned.

But when Ace met Mira, this loner had a change of heart. When Mira showed Ace that the Bakugan were more than just playthings, he agreed to join the Resistance. Ace is loyal to Mira and wasn't too happy when Dan and Marucho joined the team. But Ace warmed up when he realized what great brawlers they were.

BARON

MASTER OF: HAOS BAKUGAN

GUARDIAN BAKUGAN: NEMUS

Baron is a brawler with a lot of heart, and so when he lost Tigrerra to powerful Vexos Spectra, he was devastated. Baron became discouraged and afraid of losing his Guardian Bakugan, Nemus. But a training session with his hero, Dan, gave him new confidence.

Baron is the Battle Brawlers' biggest fan. Meeting Dan and Marucho was a real thrill, but when Baron went to Earth and met Julie and Runo, he couldn't contain his excitement. He tried to help out by working as a waiter in Runo's family restaurant, but he broke too many dishes!

MARUCHO

MASTER OF: AQUOS BAKUGAN

GUARDIAN BAKUGAN: ELFIN

Marucho may be small, but he's got enough talent to take down brawlers twice his size. He bravely fought with the Battle Brawlers to save Vestroia the first time, and when he and Dan got transported to New Vestroia he gladly joined the Resistance.

Marucho was heartbroken to learn that his guardian Bakugan, Preyas, had been captured. He wandered away from the Resistance base so he could find a new Bakugan to help him win back Preyas. There he was befriended by Elfin, an attribute-changing Bakugan, just like Preyas. Because Marucho is an expert of skill and strategy, attribute-changing Bakugan make the perfect partners for him.

MEET THE VEXOS ™

When the Vestals discovered Vestroia, they thought they had discovered a paradise. Their own planet, Vestal, was overcrowded, so they sent millions of inhabitants to colonize Vestroia, enslaving the Bakugan there and renaming the world New Vestroia.

Their leader, Prince Hydron, became obsessed with Bakugan. He decided to form a team of the best Vestal brawlers and held a series of tournaments to let the most skilled players rise to the top. He then selected the winning brawlers for each attribute: Pyrus, Aquos, Haos, Darkus, Subterra, and Ventus. This team of brawlers is called the Vexos, and they live to do Prince Hydron's bidding.

The Vexos are determined to stop the Bakugan Brawlers Resistance, whatever it takes. And Prince Hydron has charged them with one main task: to defeat and capture Dan's Drago, so that his Bakugan collection will be complete.

SPECTRA

The leader of the Vexos, Spectra is cool and composed, but he prefers to battle with the unstable fire attribute. He's supremely confident—maybe too confident—and believes he can't be beat. That makes him a strong leader, but a questionable follower of Prince Hydron.

Spectra always wears a mask, so his true identity is hidden. He uses Helios in battle, a mighty black and red Dragonoid. Spectra thinks that his Helios is the ultimate Dragonoid—until he battles Dan and his Drago. From that moment on, Spectra vows to win Drago for himself.

MYLENE

Although Spectra is the leader of the Vexos, Mylene doesn't trust him. She's got a powerful personality and believes that she would be a better leader for the group.

At least she has the battle skills to back up her boasting. Like Marucho, Mylene uses skill and strategy rather than pure power to win battles. Her Guardian Bakugan, Elico, can change attributes in play. This leaves most of her opponents dazed, confused — and beaten in the end.

GUS

MASTER OF: SUBTERRA BAKUGAN
GUARDIAN BAKUGAN: PREMO VULCAN

Like most Subterra brawlers, Gus relies on the strength and power of his Bakugan when he battles. He relies on his Premo Vulcan to smash his opponents on the field.

Premo Vulcan is a towering giant, but Gus is slim and quick. He spends his spare time training so that he can think fast in tough situations. It's those skills that allowed him to beat Dan and Drago in a battle on New Vestroia. Later, Mira took on Gus, and the two Subterra brawlers traded blows in a fairly even match. In the end, Mira won the battle—with a little help from the original Subterra master, Julie.

SHADOW

With his wild silver hair, red eyes, fangs, and purple trench coat, Shadow looks like some kind of space age vampire. You can tell just by looking at him that he prefers the dark of night to the light of day. He skillfully defeats his opponents with the sinister Darkus Bakugan on his team.

Shadow is a young Vestal nobleman, but his behavior is anything but noble. He's vicious and cruel, and he shows no mercy to those who face him on the field. Hades is not a real Bakugan at all, but a mechanical Bakugan created to carry out Shadow's evil attacks. Shadow used Hades to take down one of the most powerful brawlers ever, Shun.

MASTER OF: VENTUS BAKUGAN

GUARDIAN BAKUGAN: ALTAIR

It's no wonder Lync prefers Ventus Bakugan— he's full of hot air. He likes to talk a big game, but Lync's brawling doesn't always measure up. He wears a long cloak to conceal his battle maneuvers, but before long anyone can see what he's really made of.

The only time Lync is really dangerous is when he battles with Altair. This mechanical Bakugan was invented by Mira's father, Professor Clay, and at first appears to be indestructible.

VOLT

Volt is short and stocky, like a wrestler, which might help to explain his battle style. He's intelligent and well spoken off the field, but on the field he relies on strength, not brains, to win.

Like his sometime battle partner Lync, Volt uses a mechanical Bakugan created by Professor Clay. Brontes is a strong Bakugan, but so far the only member of the Resistance Volt has been able to defeat is Marucho.

The leader of the Vestals is a spoiled brat who is used to getting his way. When he doesn't get what he wants, he gets angry.

What Prince Hydron wants most of all is to complete his collection of Bakugan. He captured the most powerful Bakugan of each attribute: Skyress, Tigrerra, Gorem, Preyas, and Hydranoid. Only one Bakugan is missing: Dan's Dragonoid, Drago.

Prince Hydron keeps the captured Bakugan petrified, like bronze statues, so he can view them for his amusement. He's cruel and selfish, and he'll do anything to get what he wants—but mostly, he uses the Vexos to do his dirty work for him.

THE SIX ATTRIBUTES

Prince Hydron is obsessed with collecting the strongest Bakugan of each attribute. Bakugan get an attribute from one of the six planets of Vestroia. The different powers of the planets give Bakugan specialized strengths.

PYRUS

The red Bakugan are all from the Pyrus planet. Pyrus is found at the inner core of the Bakugan universe. It is from its fierce heat and within the deep recesses of molten rock that the red Bakugan draw their extraordinary strength and intensity. With unrelenting attacks from every angle, these fiery beasts rain down a firestorm — leaving their enemies in the dust.

HAOS

The white Bakugan are all from the Haos planet. The radiant planet of Haos is like the crown jewel, overwhelming any who dare gaze upon it. These Bakugan draw their strength from the immense source of power found at the planet's core. With this power, these monsters have mastered the rare and unique ability to manipulate and control light and energy, leaving their opponents dazed and confused.

VENTUS

The green Bakugan are all from the Ventus planet. Their planet is swift and silent, containing the very powerful and fast Ventus Bakugan. Any trespassers who dare cross into their borders are punished by a vicious, overwhelming cyclone. There is no escape once enemies are caught in the eye of the storm.

AQUOS

The blue Bakugan are all from the Aquos planet. Buried deep below a blanket of dark waters, a deceiving air of tranquility fills Aquos. On the surface all appears calm and still, but in that silence lurks deadly warriors, proficient in all saturated environments. These Bakugan seamlessly glide from one attack position to the next, constantly preparing for their moment of glory.

SUBTERRA

The brown Bakugan are all from the Subterra planet. They are rock solid and rugged to the core. These Bakugan are truly the toughest and mightiest warriors. They are enthusiastic battlers who give their all to crush their opponents.

DARKUS

The black Bakugan are all from the Darkus planet. Their planet is found on the dark side of the Bakugan universe. Darkus Bakugan thrive on battles hidden in the shadows, for this is where they draw their strength.

WARRIORS OF NEW VESTROIA

When the Bakugan first fell to Earth, Dan and his friends encountered many of them. They met new Bakugan in their travels, and when they faced new opponents.

After Drago saved Vestroia, all of the Bakugan warriors returned home. Dan said good-bye to his Bakugan friends, knowing he might never see them again.

When Dan was transported to New Vestroia, he realized he was about to experience a whole new world of Bakugan. Dan met Bakugan that he had never seen before. Some were created in the sinister lab of Professor Clay. Dan even saw a whole new type of Bakugan called Trap Bakugan.

Bakugan Traps come in different shapes, like a pyramid or cylindrical shape. A Bakugan Trap can be used in battle with Bakugan of the same attribute that are already on the field. The Bakugan Trap can merge with the Bakugan on the field and, often, help a brawler gain the upper hand in a match.

On these pages you'll learn everything you need to know about the Bakugan of New Vestroia. Which one do you want on your team?

ALTAIR

Appearance:

A large mechanical dragon with a long, curved tail and gleaming metal horns.

Battle Style:

Altair begins a brawl with a fierce battle cry that deafens its opponents. It then attacks with its sharp-as-swords fangs and horns while it blasts out white-hot steam from its mouth.

Where You've Seen It:

Lync Volan uses a Ventus Altair to battle against the Bakugan Brawlers Resistance.

What You Should Know:

Mira's father, Professor Clay, created Altair in his lab. Altair is the first mechanical Bakugan. At first, it seemed like Altair would be impossible to beat. But Altair is a machine, and like any machine, it can break down. When Mira first battled Altair, a power overload caused it to shut down during battle. Altair has one other key weakness: Its sensors cannot keep track of multiple opponents in battle.

BALITON

APPEARANCE:

A large, powerful monster that walks on all fours. Baliton has a protective shell on his back with large spikes protruding from it, along with a large spike on top of his head. Baliton has a long tail with sharp nails on the end.

BATTLE STYLE:

Baliton is slow-moving on the field, preferring to crush a foe with his massive weight. He can swing his long tail like a baseball bat to strike opponents.

WHERE YOU'VE SEEN HIM:

Baliton is Mira's Trap Bakugan. She used Baliton to strengthen her attack against Altair when Lync first battled with the mechanical beast.

WHAT YOU SHOULD KNOW:

Baliton can merge with Wilda in battle.

BRONTES

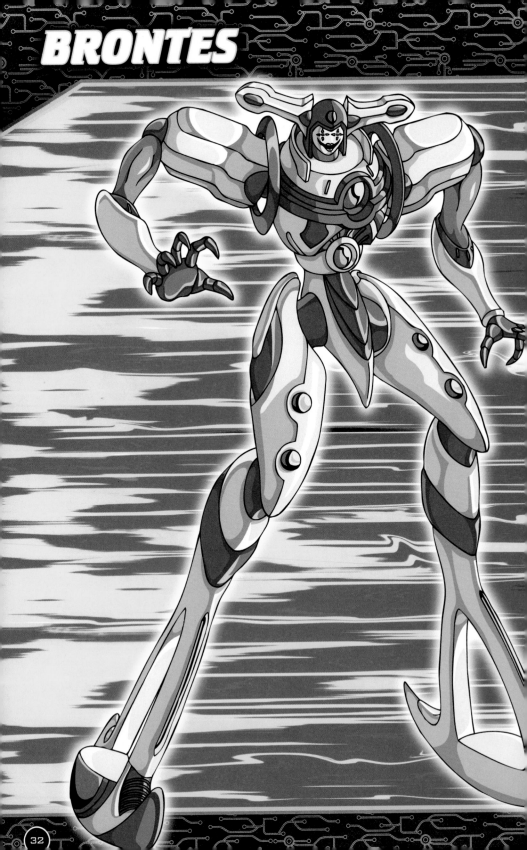

APPEARANCE:

A long and slender robot with eight arms sticking out of his head that act as a propeller. Brontes has a smiling face like a joker or a clown, with a disturbing laugh to match.

BATTLE STYLE:

Brontes has no fear. He will use forbidden abilities, which may destroy his own body, and will challenge even the strongest opponents.

WHERE YOU'VE SEEN HIM:

Vexos brawler Volt uses Brontes in battle. Volt skillfully uses Ability Cards with Brontes to shake opponents' confidence. Brontes played a big part in the battle of Volt versus Ace and Shun in the Alpha City stadium.

WHAT YOU SHOULD KNOW:

Like Altair, Brontes is a mechanical Bakugan. Brontes has no wings but can fly using the propeller on his head.

APPEARANCE:

In New Vestroia, Dragonoid looks like the Ultimate Dragonoid of Vestroia, with a green gem in his chest.

BATTLE STYLE:

Dragonoid can activate many new abilities, using power from the Perfect Core.

WHERE YOU'VE SEEN HIM:

Dragonoid has battled with Dan many times. In New Vestroia, Drago and Dan memorably battled Gus and Spectra, who wanted to capture Drago for Prince Hydron. With a little help from Shun, the Battle Brawlers triumphed over Vexos once again.

WHAT YOU SHOULD KNOW:

Drago had to leave a piece of himself behind to maintain the Infinity Core. Though this has left him a little less powerful than he once was, he is still a force to be reckoned with.

DYNAMO

APPEARANCE:
Dynamo looks like a giant robot insect, with six metal legs and a long neck. Retractable spikes can shoot out of the sides of its head.

BATTLE STYLE:
Dynamo can combine with Brontes to create Dynamo Brontes, a towering robot that's tough to take down.

WHERE YOU'VE SEEN IT:
When Marucho was lost in the desert, he was found by Vexos brawler Volt. The two engaged in a heated battle: Volt's Brontes and Dynamo versus Marucho's Elfin and the Bakugan Trap Tripod Epsilon. In the end, Dynamo helped Volt take down Marucho and his Bakugan.

WHAT YOU SHOULD KNOW:
Dynamo is a Bakugan Trap, another mechanical Bakugan created by Professor Clay.

ELFIN

APPEARANCE:
A cross between an amphibian and a fairy with a long tail, wing-like flippers, and webbed hands and feet.

BATTLE STYLE:
Elfin can choose from Aquos, Ventus, and Darkus attributes in battle. She loves to turn the tables on her opponents with a quick attribute change.

WHERE YOU'VE SEEN HER:
Marucho made a promise to himself to win back Preyas, battle the Vexos, and save New Vestroia. But he couldn't do it without a Bakugan to brawl with. While searching the woods of New Vestroia, he encountered Elfin. She refused to join him at first, but changed her mind when Mylene showed up to steal the Bakugan in the forest. Elfin and Marucho have been brawling together ever since.

WHAT YOU SHOULD KNOW:
When Elfin met Preyas, it was a perfect match. They're both outgoing and like to joke around, especially when things get tough.

APPEARANCE:

A bulky robot with the face of a human and clawed, animal-like feet. The helmet on his head makes him look like a knight in armor.

BATTLE STYLE:

Elico shoots a powerful blast of water from the golden diamond on his chest to defeat his opponents. He also wraps his six tentacles around his foes' arms and legs so they are unable to move. The six blades on his arms can be used for attack or defense.

WHERE YOU'VE SEEN HIM:

Although Mylene of Vexos chooses to brawl with brains instead of power, she often relies upon her Bakugan Elico and his brute strength. Mylene brought out Elico in her brutal battle against Resistance brawler Ace.

WHAT YOU SHOULD KNOW:

Elico is an attribute-changing Bakugan, so if you face him in battle, stay on guard. You never know what move Elico might make next.

APPEARANCE:
A large dragonfly with glowing yellow eyes and a long tail.

BATTLE STYLE:
Falcon Fly is a Bakugan Trap. It can merge with Percival in battle. When they merge, Percival rides on Falcon Fly's back and they both soar across the battlefield.

WHERE YOU'VE SEEN IT:
Ace uses Falcon Fly in battle. He teamed up Falcon Fly and Percival when he and Shun battled Volt and Lync in the Alpha City stadium.

WHAT YOU SHOULD KNOW:
Falcon Fly excels in aerial attacks.

APPEARANCE:

A mechanical, walking weapons machine with ten cannons sticking out of its arms and legs.

BATTLE STYLE:

This Bakugan Trap uses multiple attacks that make him almost unbeatable. The rockets under his feet help him to avoid enemy fire.

WHERE YOU'VE SEEN HIM:

When Shun faced Shadow in a one-on-one match, Shadow used two Bakugan created by Professor Clay: Hades and Fortress. The combined power of the two Bakugan eclipsed the power of Shun's Bakugan, and Shadow won the match.

WHAT YOU SHOULD KNOW:

Don't confuse this Fortress with the four-armed, four-faced Bakugan used by Chan on Earth. They have a similar name, but they're completely different.

APPEARANCE:

A mechanical, mythical monster with three heads, three tails, and six wings.

BATTLE STYLE:

Hades has a metal exoskeleton that protects him from attacks. In battle, he can shoot fire from each of his three heads. He can also attack opponents from many different directions using the spiked tip on the end of each of his tails. Hades may be big and heavy, but his powerful wings make him one of the fastest flying Bakugan.

WHERE YOU'VE SEEN HIM:

Shadow used Hades when he battled Shun. At the start of the battle, he tried to fool Shun into thinking that Hades was Masquerade's Bakugan Hydranoid. During the battle, "Hydranoid's" fake skin peeled off to reveal the robotic monster underneath.

WHAT YOU SHOULD KNOW:

Professor Clay used Hydranoid when he created Hades. He called his creation "the perfect blend of Bakugan and beast."

HELIOS

APPEARANCE:

A large Dragonoid with mammoth wings and a long tail ending in a vicious spike. Spikes tipped with poison cover his entire body.

BATTLE STYLE:

Helios can shoot cannonball blasts from his mouth at rapid speed.

WHERE YOU'VE SEEN HIM:

Helios is the prized Bakugan of Vexos brawler Spectra. He is just as vicious as his master, and he enters each battle hungry to win. When Spectra battled Dan for the second time, Helios decimated Drago, and Drago became Spectra's Bakugan, but not for long . . .

WHAT YOU SHOULD KNOW:

Helios is a rare and powerful Bakugan. He is known to influence fire. His ability is very powerful and he evolves quickly. This rapid evolution causes Helios to have a short life span.

HEXADOS

APPEARANCE:

Although it's made of metal, Hexados looks like a giant sandworm with a long body.

BATTLE STYLE:

Hexados can dig underground and pop up unexpectedly on its opponent's side of the battlefield. This Bakugan can also crush its foes by winding its body around them in a tight squeeze.

WHERE YOU'VE SEEN IT:

Vexos brawler Gus combined this Bakugan Trap with his Premo Vulcan in a battle against Mira. Mira used two Subterra Bakugan also: Wilda and Baliton. It was a pretty even match, but Mira's use of Subterra strategy gave her the edge.

WHAT YOU SHOULD KNOW:

Hexados has three red eyes that allow it to see all around its body, and the small blue holes along its length can shoot arrows in any direction.

HYLASH

Appearance:
A large robot warrior with large shields on his shoulders.

Battle Style:
Hylash is a Trap Bakugan. His method of attack is to spin until he defeats his opponent.

Where You've Seen Him:
Shun combines Hylash with Ingram in battle. When the two merge, Ingram rides on top of Hylash. When Shun battled Shadow, Hades blasted Hylash off the field.

What You Should Know:
Hylash has a normal mode and a special "cocoon mode" used in battle.

Appearance:
A cross between an angel and a bird of prey.

Battle Style:
Ingram can dive from the sky like an eagle to attack its opponents on the field.

Where You've Seen It:
When Shun found himself suddenly transported to New Vestroia, Cosmic Ingram was one of the first Bakugan he met. Ingram became his main Bakugan, battling with Shun the way his former Bakugan, Skyress, used to.

What You Should Know:
Bakugan Trap Hylash can merge with Ingram.

MAXUS DRAGONOID

APPEARANCE:

A huge Dragonoid combined with several weapons-focused machines to make one giant monster.

BATTLE STYLE:

This Bakugan unleashes a juggernaut of power with every attack. It can decimate an opponent with a single move.

WHAT YOU SHOULD KNOW:

Maxus Dragonoid is a combination of Drago and six different Bakugan Traps: Grakas Hound, Dark Hound, Grafias, Brachium, Spitarm, and Spyderfencer.

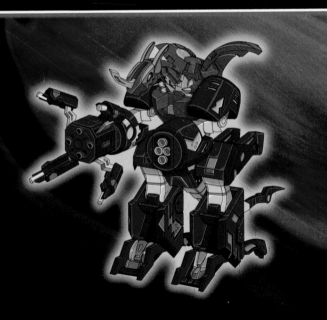

APPEARANCE:

Like Maxus Dragonoid, Maxus Helios is a massive beast made by combining Bakugan.

BATTLE STYLE:

Maxus Helios attacks with a relentless barrage of blasts.

WHAT YOU SHOULD KNOW:

Maxus Helios is composed of six Pyrus mechanical Bakugan.

MECHANICAL HELIOS

APPEARANCE:
A massive Dragonoid with wings and a body made of metal.

BATTLE STYLE:
Mechanical Helios's metal frame strengthens his defense in battle.

WHAT YOU SHOULD KNOW:
Mechanical Helios is the evolved form of Helios. To overcome his short lifespan, the powerful Helios became a cyborg — and now reigns as the supreme mechanical Bakugan.

METALFENCER

APPEARANCE:
An insectlike robot with clawed feet and a cannon on the end of each arm.

BATTLE STYLE:
This Bakugan Trap has three blue eyes that freeze its opponents so they can't strike back. It can quickly maneuver around the battlefield on its four legs, and its body can trap a foe in a tight squeeze. If all that fails, Metalfencer can end the fight with a laser blast from its tail!

WHERE YOU'VE SEEN IT:
Spectra used Metalfencer when he battled Dan for the second time. He combined Metalfencer with Helios using Battle Unit Mode. Metalfencer latched itself to Helios's body, forming an impenetrable shield of armor and equipping Helios with added weapons.

WHAT YOU SHOULD KNOW:
Metalfencer may have helped Spectra take down Drago, but the Bakugan Apollonir easily defeated Metalfencer in another battle.

NEMUS

APPEARANCE:

An Egyptian king in gold and blue armor. The massive wings on his back are as sharp as blades.

BATTLE STYLE:

Nemus uses his wrist guards to deflect attacks. He carries a long staff that can shoot a beam of light at his opponents.

WHERE YOU'VE SEEN HIM:

After Bakugan Brawlers Resistance fighter Baron lost Tigrerra to the Vexos, he lost all his confidence. Then Vexos Shadow came around looking for a brawl. Baron and Nemus stood up to Shadow and won the battle—and Baron got his confidence back.

WHAT YOU SHOULD KNOW:

Only Nemus can use the Ability Card Shade Cocoon. It shuts down all of his opponent's abilities.

PERCIVAL

APPEARANCE:

A wicked monster with unbreakable horns coming out of his head and shoulders. Percival wears a long cape and has dragon-head wristguards. He can use the cape to become invisible.

BATTLE STYLE:

The armor-plated steel on his body protects him from attacks, but Percival can also deliver some strong offense. He can shoot plasma bullets from his three mouths and take down challengers with a black tornado burning with purple sparks.

WHERE YOU'VE SEEN HIM:

Bakugan Brawlers Resistance member Ace uses a Darkus Percival in battle. When Dan joined the Resistance, Ace wanted Dan to prove himself. Percival and Dan's Drago battled for more than three hours, until the brawl finally ended in a tie.

WHAT YOU SHOULD KNOW:

Percival is a silent, mysterious creature, but has a special bond with Ace. He enjoys a heated battle, but fights without showing emotion or mercy.

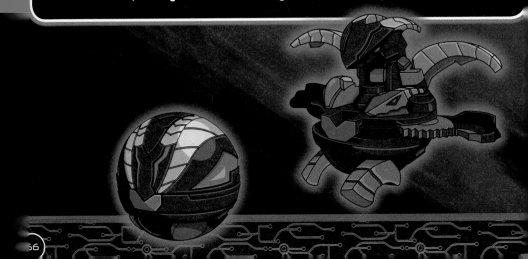

PIERCIAN

APPEARANCE:

A giant robot made of metal blocks. Huge shields cover Piercian's arms.

BATTLE STYLE:

This Bakugan Trap is a master of defense. Almost nothing can get past Piercian's shields. Ability Cards can help make Piercian's defenses even stronger.

WHERE YOU'VE SEEN IT:

When loud-mouthed brawler Lync faced Baron, he brought out his sophisticated mechanical Bakugan, Altair and Wired. Baron combined the powers of Nemus and Piercian to send Lync's metal beasts to the junkyard.

WHAT YOU SHOULD KNOW:

Piercian can change the shape of its body to create defensive barriers of different sizes and shapes.

PREMO VULCAN

APPEARANCE:

A mighty armored warrior with horns coming out of each side of his helmet. Premo Vulcan's massive fists are his biggest feature.

BATTLE STYLE:

Premo Vulcan's fists can detach and shoot at an opponent like cannonballs or missiles.

WHERE YOU'VE SEEN HIM:

Gus used his Premo Vulcan when he battled Dan for the first time. He defeated Drago—but not by enough points to capture Dan's Bakugan. Gus was proud that he won the battle, but Prince Hydron was angry that his prize was not captured.

WHAT YOU SHOULD KNOW:

Premo Vulcan can be combined with the Bakugan Trap Hexados.

SCORPION

APPEARANCE:
Just like you might expect, this Bakugan looks like a scorpion, with pincers and a long tail.

BATTLE STYLE:
Scorpion towers over the competition—literally. He can use his six legs to rise up over his enemy, putting him in the perfect position to snap his deadly, pointed tail.

WHERE YOU'VE SEEN HIM:
Dan links Scorpoin with Dragonoid to perform deadly attacks.

WHAT YOU SHOULD KNOW:
Scorpion's exoskeleton shell protects his insides from damage during battle.

APPEARANCE:

A large frog with bulging eyes and tribal markings on its face and body. Tripod Epsilon holds a long green stem with a leaf on top. A tiny snail rests on the leaf.

BATTLE STYLE:

Like a frog, this Bakugan Trap can go far with just a mighty leap. Its unusual coloring allows it to blend in with its surroundings so it can't be targeted.

WHERE YOU'VE SEEN IT:

Marucho used Elfin and Aquos Tripod Epsilon when he battled Volt. Volt merged Brontes and Dynamo into Dynamo Brontes—it was a challenging battle.

WHAT YOU SHOULD KNOW:

Tripod Epsilon might look weird, but don't understimate its power. It can use its big green eyes to control its opponent's actions.

APPEARANCE:

A warrior knight wearing heavy armor and carrying a sharp trident.

BATTLE STYLE:

This Bakugan Trap has an ability to drain an opponent of its Aquos, Ventus, or Darkus powers.

WHERE YOU'VE SEEN HIM:

Mylene sent out her Stug to try to defeat and capture Elfin, but they were no match for Marucho's new friend, an attribute-changing Aquos Bakugan. Then Mylene brought out Tripod Theta, and it looked like Elfin might lose. Only a bold defensive move from Marucho saved Elfin.

WHAT YOU SHOULD KNOW:

Tripod Theta is a legendary warrior brought back to existence by Mylene.

APPEARANCE:

An emormous Bakugan with boulder-like arms and legs.

BATTLE STYLE:

Wilda uses her powerful body to pound the ground and shake up her opponents before finishing them with a karate chop.

WHERE YOU'VE SEEN HER:

Wilda is Mira's guardian Bakugan. The first time Dan and Marucho met Mira they were amazed when she activated two abilities at the same time while brawling with Wilda.

WHAT YOU SHOULD KNOW:

Wilda may be powerful, but she's not very fast, due to her immense size.

WIRED

APPEARANCE:

A robotic bird with a long beak. This Bakugan can transform into something resembling a sleek fighting jet.

BATTLE STYLE:

Wired swoops down to attack its opponents with its indestructible beak, the sharp claws on its feet, and the bladelike feathers on its wings. Small and agile, it can easily dodge attacks.

WHERE YOU'VE SEEN IT:

Professor Clay created Wired as the perfect Bakugan to use with his mechanical masterpiece, Altair. Vexos Lync uses them both in battle.

WHAT YOU SHOULD KNOW:

Wired's super-sharp talons can shred almost any foe.

PIONEERING WARRIORS

Time to rewind: Before the Vestals came to New Vestroia, a great battle was held to save Vestroia and Earth. These Bakugan warriors played an important part in that battle. In New Vestroia, some are captured, some have changed form—and one is gone forever.

NAGA

APPEARANCE:
A colossal dragon with tattered wings and a body that looks like a skeleton.

BATTLE STYLE:
This power-hungry Bakugan will do anything to win a battle.

WHERE YOU'VE SEEN HIM:
Naga opened up the portal between Earth and Vestroia when he tried to obtain the power sources of Vestroia for himself. A huge explosion rocked the universe, and Naga ended up absorbing the negative energy of the Silent Core. He recruited Masquerade and Hal-G to help him find the location of the Infinity Core, so he could finally obtain ultimate power over Vestroia and Earth. In the end, a power overload ended Naga's reign of terror for good.

ULTIMATE DRAGONOID

EVOLUTION

DRAGONOID

APPEARANCE:

A huge winged Dragonoid with claws on his hands and feet.

BATTLE STYLE:

When Ultimate Dragonoid evolved from Delta Dragonoid, his wings grew twice the size to give him extra speed in battle. He can startle opponents with a surprise attack by firing invisible energy balls at them.

WHERE YOU'VE SEEN HIM:

Ultimate Dragonoid is one of the many forms of Dan's Drago.

DELTA DRAGONOID   ULTIMATE DRAGONOID

PREYAS ANGELO

APPEARANCE:
A combination between Preyas, a sea creature with webbed feet, and an angel. Preyas Angelo has shining white wings on his back and two smaller ones on the back of his legs and forearms.

BATTLE STYLE:
Preyas Angelo shows mercy to his opponents.

WHERE YOU'VE SEEN HIM:
Marucho's Preyas doesn't evolve like other Bakugan. He lays an egg that is half-Angelo, half-Diablo. The form Preyas will take is determined by which side of the egg is facing up.

EVOLUTION

PREYAS

PREYAS DIABLO

APPEARANCE:
Preyas Diablo has long horns on the top of his head, leathery wings, fiercesome fangs, and sharp spikes all over his body.

BATTLE STYLE:
Preyas Diablo likes to dole out fiery justice in battle. His appetite for destruction has no limits.

WHERE YOU'VE SEEN HIM:
Along with Preyas Angelo, Preyas Diablo is one of the two forms of Preyas.

PREYAS ANGELO

PREYAS DIABLO

DUAL HYDRANOID

APPEARANCE:

A two-headed dragon with sharp spikes on his back and wicked claws. Dual Hydranoid has two tails. The blades of a circular saw protrude from his chest.

BATTLE STYLE:

Fierce. Every time Dual Hydranoid defeats an opponent, he gains energy.

WHERE YOU'VE SEEN HIM:

Masquerade used Hydranoid to take on the Battle Brawlers of Earth. After he defeated his minions, Chan, Julio, Klaus, Komba, and Billy, Hydranoid gained enough power to evolve into Dual Hydranoid.

EVOLUTION

HYDRANOID

ALPHA HYDRANOID

APPEARANCE:

A three-headed winged dragon with metal armor plates protecting his body.

BATTLE STYLE:

Alpha Hydranoid's fire blasts can melt even the strongest elements.

WHERE YOU'VE SEEN HIM:

Alpha Hydranoid is the third step in the evolution of Hydranoid, a one-headed Dragonoid. Alpha Hydranoid evolved when he battled with Dan and Drago to help save Vestroia from destruction. Later, he became the Guardian Bakugan of Masquerade.

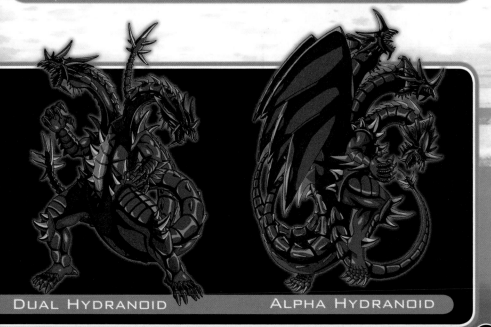

DUAL HYDRANOID   ALPHA HYDRANOID

THE SIX ANCIENT WARRIORS OF VESTROIA

These ancient Bakugan have been charged with protecting Vestroia from harm. When the Vestals colonized the planet and enslaved the Bakugan, the six soldiers freed Drago from the Perfect Core and charged him with saving Vestroia from the invaders.

Apollonir is the leader of the six legendary Bakugan. He is a cross between a Dragonoid and a Humanoid. When Dan loses Drago to Spectra in New Vestroia, Apollonir teams up with him to save his friend.

Lars Lion is a shining warrior who wears a long, white cape with gold markings. Lars Lion always tries to do what is fair and right. He uses a special weapon to retrieve fallen Haos Bakugan.

Frosch is a giant frog with a white beard, and the wisest of all the legendary soldiers. He is an expert in battle strategy. On the field, Frosch can produce a tornado to blow his enemies away.

Clayf is a towering stone giant and is the strongest of the legendary warriors. The big axe in his hand doubles as a shield. In battle, Clayf can absorb any abilities given to his opponents.

Oberus has a beak-shaped head and multiple butterfly wings that allow him to harness the power of wind. Compassion is his strongest quality. On the field, he can call upon huge power boosts to decimate his foes, but he can only defeat one opponent at a time.

Exedra is an eight-headed snake with powerful jaws in his chest. Foes on the field run from his destructive fire blasts. Exedra is able to take power from a teammate to increase his strength in battle.

LET'S

Dan and his friends are battling on New Vestroia, and that means there are a whole new set of rules. The Vestals have streamlined the game and made it easier to figure out who's winning, thanks to their gauntlets. If you want to compete on New Vestroia, you need to master these rules!

When Bakugan come to the human world, they lose their warrior form. They transform, but inside each ball is a warrior waiting to get out.

To free your Bakugan warrior, you must shoot the ball onto the playing field. When the ball stops on a Gate Card, it should open up, revealing your warrior. When this happens, your Bakugan "stands."

When your Bakugan stands, you can see a number inside the ball. This number is your Bakugan's G- Power. It's an important number. When you play Bakugan, the player with the most G-Power wins the brawl. Don't worry if your Bakugan has low G-Power. Your Bakugan can get more G-Power from Ability and Gate cards.

BRAWL!

GATE CARDS

These cards form the Bakugan playing field. There are three types of Gate cards, and you'll need one of each to play. These cards are played between the players in the area called The Field.

Each Gate card has a common back that shows the logo. On the other side, there are two important areas. The first area is the column of attribute symbols along the left-hand side of the card. In a battle, you and your opponent will match the attributes of your Bakugan with the number in the matching attribute circle on the card. You'll add that number to your Bakugan's G-Power.

The second section to pay close attention to is the text box at the bottom of the card. This text can change the game in a major way — anything listed in this section of the card overrides the regular rules of the game.

The three types of Gate Cards can be identified by their frame colors: silver, copper, and gold. You'll need one of each color in order to start your game of Bakugan.

SILVER:

These cards are some of the easiest to play. They usually don't have any instructions, but they can give your Bakugan a nice attribute bonus!

COPPER:

These cards are particularly useful when you're playing with a low G-Powered Bakugan. They can help players come from behind in all sorts of interesting ways.

GOLD:

These cards are almost always best when used with a particular Bakugan. In many cases, the card is even named after the Bakugan it benefits. If you pick a Gold Gate card that mentions a specific Bakugan, be sure to include that Bakugan in your force if you can!

ABILITY CARDS

Ability cards don't have metal on the inside. They come in three colors; blue, red and green, and you'll need one of each to play. When used wisely, Ability cards can change a game completely! Make sure to pay close attention to the text box on each card—it contains instructions, including when in a game the card can be played.

BLUE CARDS:

Blue-framed Ability cards are usually played during battle and often provide an attribute boost for your Bakugan. Like all Ability cards, the first sentence tells you when to play the card, and the rest of the text box tells you what the card does.

BATHED IN LIGHT™

80

80

Play during a battle. Your Bakugan™ gets G-Power based on its Attribute. If you are battling against a Pyrus or Darkus Bakugan, your Bakugan gets an additional +100 G-Power.

A jouer pendant un combat. Ton Bakugan™ obtient de la Puissance G selon son Attribut. Si tu combats un Bakugan Pyrus ou Darkus, ton Bakugan obtient +100 de Puissance G supplémentaire.

RAINBOW PRISM™

Play at the beginning of the game. While this is the only Ability card in your used pile, you may reroll one Aquos, Haos or Ventus once per turn.

A jouer au début de la partie. Tant que c'est la seule carte Capacité dans ta pile utilisée, tu peux relancer un Aquos, Haos ou Ventus une fois à chaque tour.

BA465-AB-SM-GBL-26 Bakugan™ Spin Master Ltd. ©2008 Sega Toys/Spin Master Ltd. 26/48i

RED CARDS:

Red-framed Ability cards usually don't include an attribute bonus, but they can still make things very interesting! These cards are usually played before or after you roll. If you're new to playing Bakugan, you might want to select one that will allow you to roll again. If you're an advanced player, you could try a card that will reward you for your rolling accuracy.

GREEN CARDS:

These are wild cards! Some are played when rolling, some during battle, and some after battles. Some have attribute boosts, others don't. They are unique, and often only usable for very specific situations. If you're a Bakugan beginner, try green Ability cards that match your Bakugan's attribute.

RAIN OF SHADOWS™

Play during a battle if you have a Darkus or Aquos Bakugan™ on an opponent's Gate. Your opponent's Bakugan gets no Attribute bonuses from the Gate.

A jouer pendant un combat si tu as un Bakugan^MC Darkus ou Aquos sur une Portail d'un adversaire. Le Bakugan de ton adversaire n'obtient aucun bonus d'Attribut de Portail.

'BA483-AB-SM-GBL-44 Bakugan™ Spin Master Ltd. ©2008 Sega Toys/Spin Master Ltd. 44/48i

GAME PLAY

To play, you need at least two players, and three Bakugan, three Gate cards, and three Ability cards each. You must have one of each type of Gate card (silver, copper, and gold) and one of each type of Ability card (blue, red, and green). The first player to collect three Gate cards in his or her used pile is the winner!

STEP 1: BEGIN

For a game with two players, sit facing one another across the battlefield. Each player should create a space on the right for unused Gate cards, Ability cards, and Bakugan (the "unused pile"), and a space on the left for used Gate cards, Ability cards, and Bakugan (the "used pile"). Each player selects one Gate card and places it facedown in the middle of the battlefield, on the side closest to his or her opponent.

STEP 2: SHOOT

The youngest player goes first—that's Player 1. Player 1 shoots a Bakugan. Make sure your Bakugan is two card lengths away from the facedown card. Then roll your Bakugan onto the field. Player 1 also has the option of playing an Ability card before shooting. Each Ability card indicates when it can be played: before, during, or after a battle.

STEP 3: BRAWL!

Player 2 shoots a Bakugan. Player 1 and Player 2 take turns until they each have a Bakugan standing on the same Gate card. Then it's time to brawl! Flip over the Gate card. Look at the number showing on each Bakugan. That number tells you how many Gs each Bakugan has.

What Happens If . . .
. . . one player has two Bakugan stand on the same card? If there are two Gate cards on the field, the player can decide which Bakugan to move to the other Gate card. If there is only one Gate card on the field, the player automatically captures the card.

STEP 4: CARD EFFECTS

If the Gate card has any text on it, do whatever it says. Then players may play any of their Ability cards in their unused pile that are playable during battle, applying whatever effects they might have. After playing an Ability card, it is moved to the player's used pile. When both players have played all the Ability cards they want, move on to step 5.

STEP 5: GATE CARD G-POWER BOOST

Each Bakugan adds the Gate Card G-Power Boost that matches the Bakugan's attribute to their Bakugan's current G-Power. These attribute bonuses are found in the six circles on the left hand side of the Gate card.

STEP 6: WINNING

The Bakugan with the highest G-power after the Gate Card G-Power Boost wins the battle. The winner moves the Gate card and their own Bakugan to their used pile. The other player moves their Bakugan to their own used pile. BAKUGAN NEVER GO TO YOUR OPPONENTS USED PILE! (And no, your friend doesn't get to keep your defeated Bakugan after the game either!)

What Happens If . . .
. . . there is a tie? The player who rolled onto the card first automatically wins!

STEP 7: TAKE TURNS

End of round one! To keep playing, continue taking turns, aiming for the remaining Gate card on the field. If Player 1 was the last to roll, it's now Player 2's turn. Take turns rolling until a new battle starts, then follow the instructions from Steps 3-6.

STEP 8: NEW GATE CARDS

Once you've battled a second time, leaving no Gate cards remaining on the field, each player places another Gate card from their unused pile facedown in the middle of the field on the side closest to his or her opponent — exactly the same way as in Step 1. Then the battle continues!

What Happens If . . .
. . . one player runs out of Bakugan in their unused pile to roll? When this happens, the player closes all of their Bakugan in their used pile and moves them all to their unused pile.

STEP 9: THE WINNER!

Keep playing until one player has three Gate cards in his or her used pile. That player is the winner. Congratulations!

BAKUGAN TRAPS

In addition to basic play with Gate cards, Ability cards, and Bakugan, New Vestroia has introduced an exciting new aspect to game play: Bakugan Traps. These major game-changers can be the difference between victory and defeat, so it is worth learning to use them!

In each Bakugan game, one trap can be used along with the three Bakugan.

Traps start in the unused pile with the other Bakugan. A trap may be played in any battle as long as you have a Bakugan in the battle and the trap is the same attribute as the Bakugan in play.

When the trap is dropped onto the Gate card, it will pop open and reveal one or more attribute icons. The player can then switch the attribute of the Bakugan to any of the new attributes revealed!

After the battle, the trap is moved into the used pile.

If a player must move Bakugan from the used pile to the un-used pile in order to have a Bakugan to roll, any trap in the used pile can be moved to the unused pile as well.

TRAP SPECIAL CARDS

In addition to the basic trap ability described above, each trap comes with a special Ability card. It isn't necessary to use the Ability card, but some are very powerful, and it's worth taking a look to see if they can help out in battle.

NEW VESTROIA'S BEST BRAWLS

The Battle Brawlers have participated in some exciting brawls on New Vestroia. Sometimes they feel the thrill of victory, and other times they suffer the agony of defeat. Check out these exciting battles. Which is your favorite?

MIRA VS. GUS

Mira and Gus both specialize in Subterra Bakugan, so this was a battle of Subterra strategy. Mira had the edge—thanks to some tips from the original Subterra master, Dan's friend Julie.

The most exciting moment after this battle came at the end, when Mira won. Spectra agreed to remove his mask and show her his face. Mira was shocked to see that her suspicions were correct—Vexos leader Spectra was really her long-lost brother, Keith!

BARON VS. SHADOW

Baron is a brawler with a big heart and a lot of energy. He wants nothing more than to save the New Vestroia Bakugan. He was honored when Haos Tigrerra chose to battle with him—and then devastated when he lost Tigrerra in a battle against Spectra.

Spectra sent Shadow to face Baron next. Baron lost the first two rounds because he was too afraid of losing his favorite Bakugan, Nemus. Then he gained confidence and fought back with strength and skill.

Shadow had three Bakugan on the field. Their combined points were almost 1,000 more Gs than Nemus. It looked like Nemus was doomed, until Baron made a brilliant move. He used the Fusion Ability Card Closed Skylight. Baron's Bakugan switched points with Shadow. Baron won all three Bakugan in one move—and even more importantly, he won their freedom.

MARUCHO VS. MYLENE

Cruel Mylene loves to fly her spaceship over New Vestroia, capturing helpless Bakugan. When she flew over the woods protected by Elfin, Elfin agreed to battle with Marucho and stop Mylene.

It was three Bakugan against one. Mylene's Aquos Abis Omega and Aquos Stug battled Elfin. Elfin kept them on their toes by changing attributes during the battle. Elfin had the upper hand, until Mylene used the Bakugan Trap Aquos Tripod Theta to revive her fallen Bakugan.

Elfin was almost knocked out by Tripod Theta's Octo Whip ability, but Marucho activated her defenses just in time. He got knocked out by a tidal wave of power, and Mylene thought she had won after all. But a mysterious brawler emerged from the shadows and sent Mylene and her Bakugan packing. Later, Marucho would learn his rescuer was his good friend Shun.

SHUN AND ACE VS. LYNC AND VOLT

When Shun and Ace entered the Bakugan tournament in Alpha City stadium, it wasn't because they wanted a prize. They were keeping the Vexos busy while Dan, Mira, and Marucho tried to destroy the Dimension Controller located in the city.

The four-man battle is memorable for its many twists and turns. Shun and Ace string along Lync and Volt for as long as they can to buy their friends some time. But then Lync merges Wired with Altair to create a devastating battle machine. Luckily, Shun figures out that Altair's sensors can't keep track of multiple opponents. He and Ace barrage Altair with their Bakugan. When Percival uses Misty Shadow to transform into a flock of bats, it drives Altair batty, and the Bakugan has a mechanical meltdown.

Just in time, Dan and the others destroy the Dimension Controller. The Vestals in the stands are first frightened to see the Bakugan on the loose, but then stunned when they realize the Bakugan can talk. It's an important step in saving New Vestroia.

SHUN VS. SHADOW

Ace and Marucho were captured. Dan, Mira, and Baron were stuck on Earth. Shun was the only brawler left to face the Vexos.

Shun and Shadow battled it out, Western style, on a deserted street in the dark. Shadow started out with a Bakugan he called Mechanical Hydranoid, but Shun quickly realized they were dealing with a whole new Bakugan: the sinister robot, Hades. Shun knew he might not be able to stand up against Hades' awesome power and almost gave up the fight. In a touching moment, Ingram told Shun not to worry—he'd always be by his side, no matter what.

In the end, Shun's fears were right. Hades overcame Ingram, and Shun was captured by the Vexos.

DAN VS. SPECTRA

After Spectra beat Dan, he captured Drago and turned him into a black Dragonoid corrupted by Negative Energy. One of the Six Legendary Bakugan Warriors, Apollonir, arrived to help Dan save Drago.

During the battle, Spectra used forbidden cards to steal energy from the Perfect Core. Blinded by greed and power, Spectra did not see the danger Drago was in. Dan knew he needed to do something desperate to save Drago. He had one shot: to pitch Apollonir into Drago's chest so Apollonir could absorb the extra energy. If Dan missed, Dan could end up destroying Drago, and New Vestroia would split up into six different worlds once more.

But Dan's aim was spot on, and Drago was restored to his old self. Dan was happy to get his best friend back! But there were still many captured Bakugan to be saved.

YOUR BAKUGAN

Whether you want to master strategy like Marucho or brawl with brawn like Dan, the best thing you can do is to know your Bakugan's strengths and weaknesses. Use these pages to write down info about your Bakugan when you get them. Before you brawl, check out your stats to plan your strategy.

BAKUGAN NAME: _MAXUS HELIOS_

ATTRIBUTE: _IN GRAM_

GATE CARDS TO USE WITH THIS BAKUGAN: _____
MAXUS DRAGONOT

ABILITY CARDS TO USE WITH THIS BAKUGAN: _____
_____

WINS: ⬤○○○○○○○○○○○○○○○○○○○○○○○○○○○○○○○○○○○○○○

LOSES: ○○○○○○○○○○○○○○○○○○○○○○○○○○○○○○○○○○○○○○

BAKUGAN NAME: _____

ATTRIBUTE: _____

GATE CARDS TO USE WITH THIS BAKUGAN: _____
_____

ABILITY CARDS TO USE WITH THIS BAKUGAN: _____
_____

WINS: ○○○○○○○○○○○○○○○○○○○○○○○○○○○○○○○○○○○○○○

LOSES: ○○○○○○○○○○○○○○○○○○○○○○○○○○○○○○○○○○○○○○

BAKUGAN NAME: _____

ATTRIBUTE: _____

GATE CARDS TO USE WITH THIS BAKUGAN: _____

_____

ABILITY CARDS TO USE WITH THIS BAKUGAN: _____

_____

WINS: ○○○○○○○○○○○○○○○○○○○○○○○○○○○○○○○○○○

LOSES: ○○○○○○○○○○○○○○○○○○○○○○○○○○○○○○○○○

BAKUGAN NAME: _____

ATTRIBUTE: _____

GATE CARDS TO USE WITH THIS BAKUGAN: _____

_____

ABILITY CARDS TO USE WITH THIS BAKUGAN: _____

_____

WINS: ○○○○○○○○○○○○○○○○○○○○○○○○○○○○○○○○○○○

LOSES: ○○○○○○○○○○○○○○○○○○○○○○○○○○○○○○○○○○○

BAKUGAN NAME: _____

ATTRIBUTE: _____

GATE CARDS TO USE WITH THIS BAKUGAN: _____

_____

ABILITY CARDS TO USE WITH THIS BAKUGAN: _____

_____

WINS: ○○○○○○○○○○○○○○○○○○○○○○○○○○○○○○○○○○

LOSES: ○○○○○○○○○○○○○○○○○○○○○○○○○○○○○○○○○○

BAKUGAN NAME: _____

ATTRIBUTE: _____

GATE CARDS TO USE WITH THIS BAKUGAN: _____
_____

ABILITY CARDS TO USE WITH THIS BAKUGAN: _____

WINS: ○○○○○○○○○○○○○○○○○○○○○○○○○○○○○○○○○○

LOSES: ○○○○○○○○○○○○○○○○○○○○○○○○○○○○○○○○○○

BAKUGAN NAME: _____

ATTRIBUTE: _____

GATE CARDS TO USE WITH THIS BAKUGAN: _____
_____

ABILITY CARDS TO USE WITH THIS BAKUGAN: _____
_____

WINS: ○○○○○○○○○○○○○○○○○○○○○○○○○○○○○○○○○○○

LOSES: ○○○○○○○○○○○○○○○○○○○○○○○○○○○○○○○○○○○

BAKUGAN NAME: _____

ATTRIBUTE: _____

GATE CARDS TO USE WITH THIS BAKUGAN: _____
_____

ABILITY CARDS TO USE WITH THIS BAKUGAN: _____
_____

WINS: ○○○○○○○○○○○○○○○○○○○○○○○○○○○○○○○○○○

LOSES: ○○○○○○○○○○○○○○○○○○○○○○○○○○○○○○○○○○

BAKUGAN NAME: _____

ATTRIBUTE: _____

GATE CARDS TO USE WITH THIS BAKUGAN: _____

_____

ABILITY CARDS TO USE WITH THIS BAKUGAN: _____

_____

WINS: ○○○○○○○○○○○○○○○○○○○○○○○○○○○○○○○○○○○

LOSES: ○○○○○○○○○○○○○○○○○○○○○○○○○○○○○○○○○○

BAKUGAN NAME: _____

ATTRIBUTE: _____

GATE CARDS TO USE WITH THIS BAKUGAN: _____

_____

ABILITY CARDS TO USE WITH THIS BAKUGAN: _____

_____

WINS: ○○○○○○○○○○○○○○○○○○○○○○○○○○○○○○○○○○○

LOSES: ○○○○○○○○○○○○○○○○○○○○○○○○○○○○○○○○○○

BAKUGAN NAME: _____

ATTRIBUTE: _____

GATE CARDS TO USE WITH THIS BAKUGAN: _____

_____

ABILITY CARDS TO USE WITH THIS BAKUGAN: _____

_____

WINS: ○○○○○○○○○○○○○○○○○○○○○○○○○○○○○○○○○○○

LOSES: ○○○○○○○○○○○○○○○○○○○○○○○○○○○○○○○○○○

BAKUGAN NAME: _____

ATTRIBUTE: _____

GATE CARDS TO USE WITH THIS BAKUGAN: _____

_____

ABILITY CARDS TO USE WITH THIS BAKUGAN: _____

_____

WINS: ○○○○○○○○○○○○○○○○○○○○○○○○○○○○○○○○

LOSES: ○○○○○○○○○○○○○○○○○○○○○○○○○○○○○○○○

BAKUGAN NAME: _____

ATTRIBUTE: _____

GATE CARDS TO USE WITH THIS BAKUGAN: _____

_____

ABILITY CARDS TO USE WITH THIS BAKUGAN: _____

_____

WINS: ○○○○○○○○○○○○○○○○○○○○○○○○○○○○○○○○

LOSES: ○○○○○○○○○○○○○○○○○○○○○○○○○○○○○○○○

BAKUGAN NAME: _____

ATTRIBUTE: _____

GATE CARDS TO USE WITH THIS BAKUGAN: _____

_____

ABILITY CARDS TO USE WITH THIS BAKUGAN: _____

_____

WINS: ○○○○○○○○○○○○○○○○○○○○○○○○○○○○○○○○

LOSES: ○○○○○○○○○○○○○○○○○○○○○○○○○○○○○○○○